Scarlen Martínez

The Tale of El Chiquitín

Illustrated by Vanessa Balleza

It's a chilly fall afternoon, and Rosario *está haciendo lo que más le gusta*, playing hopscotch with her friend Sissy.
Sissy doesn't seem like she's having much fun.
Can it be because Rosario has won four games in a row?!!

Rosario is worried about Sissy and decided to stop hopping around.
"Sissy, what's wrong?" asked Rosario.

Sissy looks around and whispers,
"I can't tell you or *it* might hear me."

"Sissy, don't be a sore loser. You lost all four games in a row and now you are trying to *asustarme*."

"Besides, *estamos solitas aquí*, no one is outside" said Rosario as she pointed to the empty sidewalk.

"Rosario, we are **not** alone, *el Chiquitín* is always watching and *escuchando*!" responded Sissy.

Rosario saw the fear in her friend's eyes and knew she was serious. "What's *el Chiquitín*?" asked Rosario.

The girls sat down on the curb and Sissy began to tell her friend Rosario about *el Chiquitín*; a strange and mysterious creature that has been in her house for many days.

"It gets inside your *casa* and turns your *mamá y papá* into **ZOMBIES!!!**" whispered Sissy, as she looked over her shoulder.

Sissy sat there telling her friend how it all happened.

Un día, her parents left her with her grandmother, *abuela Tita*.
They said they would be back with a surprise. But instead, they came back
with a mysterious package that made the most horrible sound.

Day and night, she heard screams coming from her parent's bedroom.
And worst of all, she barely even saw them around anymore. Her *mamá*
didn't sing with her and her *papá* didn't have time to play.

Then, *una noche*, she heard strange noise coming from the kitchen.
It was her *mamá!* Or so she thought...
As she looked closer, she saw her mom's hair was a mess.
She noticed big black circles around her eyes,
like she had not slept for years!

She looked like a **ZOMBIE!**

"My parents are **ZOMBIES** now Rosario!"
cried Sissy.

"I followed them into the kitchen and I saw them carrying bottles of milk. They walked upstairs with a hundred milk bottles!

I didn't even know my parents liked *leche* that much!

Every two hours, they would come back downstairs to grab more bottles of *leche* and take them back to their rooms!" cried Sissy.

"Sissy, stop being a drama queen! Did you try asking your abuela what's going on? I'm sure she has an explanation. *¡Ella sabe de todo!*" exclaimed Rosario.

"Of course, I asked her! And she said this is all because of *el Chiquitín*" cried Sissy. The girls tried to figure it all out. *¿Cómo fue* que Sissy's parents turned into **ZOMBIES?**

What was in that mysterious *paquete* her parents had brought home? And why did they drink so much *leche* at night??!!!

Suddenly, Rosario's mom yelled out the kitchen window,
"Rosario, *ven a cenar*, before your food gets cold!!!"

It was dinner time and the girls would have to solve this mystery another day.
Rosario felt bad for her friend but she was happy to be having a **normal** dinner
with her **normal** parents.

At dinner, the family ate Rosario's favorite food, *mangú!*

As the family ate, her father gave her mom an extra scoop.
"Make sure you eat a lot," warned her father as he piled more *mangú* on her mother's plate, "we don't want to upset *al Chiquitín.*"

Rosario's mouth dropped wide open. She couldn't believe what she had heard. Was *el Chiquitín* coming to her house too?!!

She was so worried she couldn't even finish her *mangú!*

Later that night in her room, Rosario was determined to solve this mystery. She was not going to let anyone mess with her *familia.*

She thought about all the strange things Sissy had told her during their playtime. She wrote down any clues she could think of.

Can you help Rosario figure out who or what is *"el Chiquitín"* before it's too late?

Glossary

What does this mean?

1. *está haciendo lo que más le gusta* - Is Doing what they like
2. *asustarme* - scare me
3. *solitas aquí* - alone here
4. *el Chiquitín* - the little one
5. *escuchando* - listening
6. *casa* - home
7. *mamá y papá* - mom and dad
8. *un día* - one day
9. *abuela Tita* - Grandma Tita
10. *una noche* - one night
11. *mamá* - mother
12. *leche* - milk
13. *¡Ella sabe de todo!* - She knows everything
14. *cómo fue que* - how was it that
15. *ven a cenar* - come have dinner
16. *familia* - family
17. *mañana* - tomorrow
18. *mangú* - A traditional dish of the Dominican Republic that consist of mashed green plantain.

Back cover

19. *cuando era chiquita* - when she was little

Sissy and Rosario are counting on you
to help solve the mystery of *el Chiquitín*.
What clues can you find in the story?

CPSIA information can be obtained
at www.ICGtesting.com
Printed in the USA
LVHW062021070621
689561LV00004B/550